THE STORY OF
A FIERCE BAD RABBIT

THE STORY OF
A FIERCE BAD RABBIT

BY

BEATRIX POTTER

Author of
" *The Tale of Peter Rabbit,*" *etc.*

FREDERICK WARNE

The reproductions in this book have been made using
the most modern electronic scanning methods from entirely
new transparencies of Beatrix Potter's original watercolours.
They enable Beatrix Potter's skill as an artist to be appreciated
as never before, not even during her own lifetime.

C130357013

FREDERICK WARNE

Published by the Penguin Group, 27 Wrights Lane, London W8 5TZ, England
Penguin Books USA Inc., 375 Hudson Street, New York, New York 10014, USA
Penguin Books Australia Ltd, Ringwood, Victoria, Australia
Penguin Books Canada Ltd, 10 Alcorn Avenue, Toronto, Ontario, Canada M4V 3B2
Penguin Books (NZ) Ltd, 182-190 Wairau Road, Auckland 10, New Zealand

Penguin Books Ltd, Registered Offices: Harmondsworth, Middlesex, England

First published 1906
This edition with new reproductions first published 1987

Colour reproduction by
East Anglian Engraving Company Ltd, Norwich
Printed and bound in Great Britain by
William Clowes Limited, Beccles and London

THIS is a fierce bad
'Rabbit; look at his
savage whiskers, and his
claws and his turned-up tail.

THIS is a nice gentle
Rabbit. His mother
has given him a carrot.

THE bad Rabbit would
like some carrot.

HE doesn't say "Please."
He takes it !

AND he scratches the good Rabbit very badly.

THE good Rabbit creeps away, and hides in a hole. It feels sad.

THIS is a man with a gun.

HE sees something sitting on a bench. He thinks it is a very funny bird!

HE comes creeping up
behind the trees.

AND then he shoots—
BANG!

THIS is what happens—

BUT this is all he finds on the bench, when he rushes up with his gun.

THE good Rabbit peeps
out of its hole,

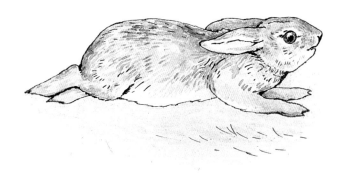

AND it sees the bad Rabbit tearing past—without any tail or whiskers!

The "PETER RABBIT" BOOKS
by BEATRIX POTTER

PETER RABBIT · SQUIRREL NUTKIN
TAILOR OF GLOUCESTER · BENJAMIN BUNNY
TWO BAD MICE · MRS. TIGGY-WINKLE
MR. JEREMY FISHER · TOM KITTEN
JEMIMA PUDDLE-DUCK · THE FLOPSY BUNNIES
MRS. TITTLEMOUSE · TIMMY TIPTOES
JOHNNY TOWN-MOUSE · MR. TOD
PIGLING BLAND · SAMUEL WHISKERS
THE PIE & THE PATTY-PAN · GINGER & PICKLES
LITTLE PIG ROBINSON

A FIERCE BAD RABBIT   MISS MOPPET
APPLEY DAPPLY'S   CECILY PARSLEY'S
NURSERY RHYMES   NURSERY RHYMES
PETER RABBIT'S   TOM KITTEN'S
PAINTING BOOK   PAINTING BOOK